# THE PRICE OF PASSION

ONESIMUS MALATJI

Copyright © 2023 ONESIMUS MALATJI

**The Price Of Passion**
**By: Onesimus  Malatji**

**Third-Party Content:**

This book may reference or include content from third-party sources. The author and publisher do not endorse or take responsibility for the accuracy or content of such third-party material.

**Endorsements:**

Any endorsement, testimonial, or representation contained in this book reflects the author's personal views and opinions. It does not imply an endorsement by any third party.
Results Disclaimer: The success stories and examples mentioned in this book are not guarantees of individual success. Actual results may vary based on various factors, including effort and circumstances.

**Results Disclaimer:**

The success stories and examples mentioned in this book are not guarantees of individual success. Actual results may vary based on various factors, including effort and circumstances.
No Guarantee of Outcome: The strategies, techniques, and advice provided in this book are based on the author's experiences and research. However, there is no guarantee that following these strategies will lead to a specific outcome or result.

**Fair Use Notice:**

This book may contain copyrighted material used for educational and illustrative purposes. Such material is used under the "fair use" provisions of copyright law.

# DEDICATION

Being one of the difficulties in my family, always stubborn, I thank God I turned out alright. I dedicate this book to my mother, Esther Malatji. I will always love you. You have raised me well until I became a fully grown man. Thank you for your prayers and support during my tough times in life. Additionally, I extend my heartfelt dedication to my beautiful wife, the partner of my life, Petunia. You have been there for me and our family, and you are truly one in a million – the best motivator. I thank God for having you as my spouse, partner, and my inspiration; you are one of my most special and wonderful gifts. During times of trials, you have never walked out on us. Thank you. I love you so much.

I also send this dedication to my brother Edward "Gong," one of the greatest creative businesspersons alive. Thank you for being a wonderful brother and supporting me in times of need and trial. May God bless you and increase your business anointing. I love you so much. Special greetings to my sister Bertha, your passion for food will undoubtedly touch the world. I love you.

Furthermore, I extend my love and dedication to my brother Mohau; I will always cherish you, brother. Special Dedication for Galetsang & Dineo I will always love you no matter what. This is also for my friends, and fellow soldiers in war: Zama, Panana, Tshwane, Blessing, Lowen, Winners I love you guys – you are my family. Special Gratitude to my inspirer my mother. I deeply respect the gift that God has put in you, and I am immensely grateful for having you while I was putting this book together.

**Thank you, my dear mother, Esther Malatji. I love you so much**

# ACKNOWLEDGMENTS

I extend my deepest gratitude to everyone who has been a part of this incredible journey, both seen and unseen. Your support, encouragement, and unwavering belief in me have been the driving force behind the creation of this book.

To my family, for standing by me through thick and thin, for believing in my dreams, and for being a constant source of inspiration – your love and encouragement have been my guiding light.

To my friends, mentors, and colleagues, your valuable insights and feedback have shaped the ideas within these pages. Your willingness to share your wisdom and experiences has enriched this work beyond measure.

To all those who have supported me on my path, whether through a kind word, a helping hand, or a moment of shared understanding, thank you. Your presence in my life has made all the difference.

To the countless individuals who have faced challenges and setbacks, yet continued to strive for greatness, your stories have fuelled the inspiration behind these words. May you find solace and encouragement within these pages.

And finally, to the readers who have embarked on this journey with me, thank you for allowing me to share my thoughts and experiences. It is my hope that this book serves as a beacon of hope, a source of guidance, and a reminder that fulfilment can be found in every step of life's intricate tapestry.

With heartfelt appreciation,


**Onesimus Malatji**

# THE PRICE OF PASSION

# THE PRICE OF PASSION

## BEGINNINGS DIVERGE

In the heart of a bustling city, where the skyline was a mosaic of towering structures and the streets hummed with unceasing activity, two girls, Julia and Maya, began their journeys in worlds as different as night and day.

Julia's world was one of opulence and excess. Nestled in the affluent suburbs, her childhood home was a grandiose testament to her parents' wealth. Her father, a successful businessman, and her mother, a socialite, provided her with every material comfort one could imagine. Yet, beneath the veneer of luxury, Julia's world was starkly empty of the warmth of parental affection. Her parents, often absent, compensated for their lack of presence with gifts and allowances, inadvertently teaching Julia that love was something to be bought and displayed.

As a child, Julia's days were filled with private tutors, elite dance classes, and extravagant birthday parties where she was the princess in a sea of admirers. But at night, in her expansive, lonely bedroom, she yearned for something more profound than the glittering jewels and designer clothes that lined her closet. The lack of genuine connections in her early years left an indelible mark on Julia, instilling in her a relentless pursuit of attention and validation through material means.

Contrastingly, several miles away in a modest neighbourhood, Maya's childhood painted a different picture. Born to a family of modest means, Maya's life was rich in love and guidance. Her parents, though not wealthy, were hardworking and devoted. Her father, a school teacher, and her mother, a nurse, imbued in Maya the values of education, hard work, and the importance of forging one's path.

Maya's home was always filled with laughter, discussions, and a sense of togetherness. Her parents, despite their busy schedules, always made time for family dinners, weekend outings, and heart-to-heart conversations.

Maya grew up understanding that true wealth was not in material possessions but in the richness of character and relationships. Her childhood, devoid of luxury but abundant in love, shaped her into a grounded, ambitious, and empathetic young woman.

As these two girls, Julia and Maya, grew up in their contrasting worlds, they unknowingly walked the paths that would lead them towards vastly different destinies. Julia, in her mansion surrounded by possessions yet void of genuine affection, and Maya, in her cosy home brimming with love and life lessons, were both beginning their divergent journeys towards understanding the true price of passion.

This sets the stage for the contrasting lives of Julia and Maya, highlighting the impact of their childhood environments and upbringing on their personalities and future choices. It creates a foundation for exploring the themes of materialism, emotional fulfilment, and the varied paths to personal satisfaction and success.

## PATHS TAKEN

As the years passed, the paths of Julia and Maya diverged further, each step reflecting the lessons and values imprinted upon them in their formative years. Julia, now a young woman of striking beauty, stepped into the world armed with the belief that her worth was intertwined with her ability to captivate and attract.

Her high school years were a blur of boyfriends, each more popular or attractive than the last. She thrived on the attention, the temporary adoration filling the void left by her emotionally distant parents. College was no different; it became yet another stage for her to seek validation. Parties, sororities, and a string of relationships defined her college experience. Academics were an afterthought, a minor inconvenience in her pursuit of admiration and love as she had come to understand it.

But with each relationship, the emptiness grew. Each breakup left a residue of disappointment and a nagging question that perhaps this wasn't the path to the happiness she sought. Yet, the fear of being alone, of being unnoticed, propelled her forward on this self-destructive trajectory.

Meanwhile, Maya's journey was starkly different. She entered college with a clear vision and unyielding determination. Her parents' sacrifices and teachings had instilled in her a deep respect for education and self-reliance.

College for Maya was not a social playground but a stepping stone to a future she was actively constructing. She immersed herself in her studies, her passion for law and justice fuelling her ambition. Her social life was a secondary concern, a distant orbit around the central sun of her academic pursuits.

While Julia attended parties and navigated the turbulent waters of romantic relationships, Maya spent her nights in the library, her days filled with lectures, internships, and student organizations. She was not without friends or fun, but these were chosen wisely, never allowed to derail her from her path.

The contrast between their lives could not have been more pronounced. Julia, caught in the whirlwind of fleeting relationships, each leaving her more jaded than the last, and Maya, steadfast in her journey, her eyes fixed on a future she was determined to shape with her own hands.

This chapter in their lives laid the foundation for the women they were becoming, setting the stage for the triumphs and tribulations that lay ahead in their search for fulfilment and identity. As college came to a close, Julia and Maya stood at the threshold of adulthood, each carrying the lessons of their past into a future that was uncertain yet brimming with potential. The paths they had taken were about to lead them to new challenges and experiences, shaping the course of their lives in ways they could scarcely imagine.

## THE PURSUIT

In the bustling city that never sleeps, Julia's pursuit for satisfaction through partners became an unending quest, a relentless journey that promised much but delivered little.

Post-college life for Julia was a continuation of her earlier years, but with higher stakes. The clubs were more exclusive, the parties more extravagant, and the men more affluent. Her beauty and charm were her currency, and she spent them lavishly, moving from one high-profile relationship to another. Each new partner offered the promise of something different, something more fulfilling than the last, but the outcome was always the same – a fleeting rush of excitement followed by an all-too-familiar emptiness.

Julia's relationships were a tapestry of society's elite – businessmen, politicians, artists. Each brought her into new circles, new experiences, and new levels of luxury. She travelled to exotic destinations, dined at the finest restaurants, and wore the most exquisite designer clothes. To the outside observer, Julia's life was one of envy – a perpetual high of glamour and excitement. But beneath the surface, Julia's reality was far from enviable. Each relationship left her feeling more hollow than before.

The initial thrill of new romance quickly gave way to the realization that these men were interested more in her beauty than her person. She was a trophy, a symbol of status, rather than a partner to be cherished and respected.

The more she pursued this path, the more she felt disconnected from herself. Julia's identity became tied to the men she dated, her self-worth fluctuating with their attention and approval. The once confident and vibrant young woman was now riddled with insecurities, her happiness tethered to the transient affections of others.

Night after night, Julia lay in bed, staring at the ceiling of her luxurious apartment, gifted by her latest beau. In these quiet moments, the truth whispered to her – this was not the life she wanted. But the fear of being alone, of facing the void without the distraction of a relationship, kept her trapped in this cycle.

Julia's pursuit of satisfaction through partners was a paradox – the more she sought fulfilment in others, the more it eluded her. She was chasing a mirage, a vision of happiness that was always just out of reach. Her journey was a poignant illustration of the age-old truth that true satisfaction cannot be found in others but must be cultivated within oneself. As Julia continued her pursuit, the city around her hummed with life, indifferent to the silent struggle of a woman lost in the labyrinth of her desires.

# A WORLD APART

As Julia navigated her tumultuous personal life, Maya entered a world that was starkly different – a world of law, order, and stability. Graduating from college with honours, she stepped confidently into her new role at a prestigious law firm. It was a world where her intellect, determination, and hard work were the currencies of success, and Maya invested them wisely.

Her days were filled with legal briefs, client meetings, and courtroom appearances. She quickly earned a reputation as a rising star in the legal community, her sharp mind and unwavering ethics setting her apart from her peers. Maya's passion for justice and fairness shone through in her work, and she found deep satisfaction in the tangible impact of her efforts.

The law firm became her second home, a place where she felt challenged and fulfilled. She thrived on the intellectual rigor of her work, and each successful case was a testament to her skill and dedication. Unlike Julia, Maya's satisfaction came not from external validation, but from the sense of accomplishment in her chosen career.

However, Maya's life was not solely defined by her career. She maintained a balanced life, nurturing friendships and hobbies. Her evenings and weekends were often spent volunteering at a local community centre, where she offered free legal advice.

This commitment to community service was rooted in her upbringing, a reflection of the values her parents had instilled in her. Maya's personal life was also a picture of stability. She had a close-knit circle of friends from college and law school, and while she dated, it was with a mindfulness and selectivity that stood in stark contrast to Julia's approach. Maya sought a partner who shared her values and ambitions, someone who would be a true companion rather than just a romantic interest.

In Maya's world, success was measured not by the opulence of one's lifestyle or the number of social media followers, but by the impact one made in their profession and community. Her life was a testament to the power of focus, hard work, and integrity.

As Maya continued to ascend the ranks of her profession, she remained grounded. She remembered where she came from and knew where she was going. Her world, a world apart from Julia's, was one of purpose and meaning, a stark contrast to the fleeting pleasures of Julia's pursuit of satisfaction through relationships.

Maya's journey was proof that stability and success need not be sacrificed for passion and ambition. In her world of law and order, she found her own kind of excitement and fulfilment, a beacon of hope and a model of possibility for young women everywhere.

## SHADOWS OF DOUBT

As the seasons changed in the vibrant city, so too did the currents of Julia's life. The glamour that once seemed so alluring now began to lose its sheen. With each passing relationship and each superficial connection, Julia found herself enveloped in growing shadows of doubt about the lifestyle she had chosen.

It was during a quiet evening, in her elegantly furnished apartment filled with tokens of her past relationships, that Julia's introspection deepened. Surrounded by luxury but engulfed in solitude, she pondered over the countless faces and names that had come and gone in her life. None had left a lasting impact on her heart, only fleeting imprints that faded as quickly as they appeared.

The realization hit her with unexpected force. The life she was living, once a dream, now felt like an unending cycle of emptiness. The parties, the dinners, the jet-set vacations that filled her social media feeds, were they truly what she wanted? Or were they just a facade, a mask she wore to hide the void within?

For the first time, Julia began to question the choices that had led her to this point. She thought back to her childhood, to the moments when her parents' absence was filled with gifts instead of love and guidance.

Had she been seeking the same in her adult relationships? Was her pursuit of attention and affection through partners simply a continuation of that childhood yearning for genuine connection?

These questions lingered in her mind, casting long shadows over her once unshakable confidence in her way of life. The men she dated, once symbols of success and desirability, now seemed like mere distractions from the deeper issues she had long ignored.

As she sat alone, the city lights twinkling in the distance, Julia felt a profound sense of loneliness. It was not the absence of people that troubled her; her life was full of acquaintances and admirers. It was a more profound loneliness; born of a realization that she had been living without truly knowing herself or what she genuinely desired from life.

In this moment of introspection, Julia's journey took a pivotal turn. The shadows of doubt that had crept into her life were not just obstacles to be overcome; they were signposts, pointing towards a path of self-discovery and genuine fulfilment.

She knew that this path would not be easy, that it would require her to confront truths she had long avoided, but for the first time, Julia felt a flicker of hope, a sense that there was more to life than the pursuit of fleeting pleasures.

The night wore on, and the city slept, but for Julia, it was as if she had awakened from a long slumber. The shadows of doubt, while daunting, beckoned her towards a journey of transformation, a journey to find the true Julia that lay hidden beneath the layers of expectation and illusion.

# A SOLID FOUNDATION

In the heart of the bustling metropolis, while Julia grappled with her inner turmoil, Maya's life was on an upward trajectory, her career in law beginning to flourish. The solid foundation she had built during her academic years now bore fruit in the form of recognition, success, and a sense of true accomplishment.

Maya's days were a whirlwind of activity, each filled with new challenges and opportunities. Her reputation as a sharp, ethical lawyer grew rapidly. Her firm entrusted her with more significant, high-profile cases, and she tackled each with a blend of passion and precision that was rare in her field. Her success was not just in the courtroom victories, but also in the respect she earned from her colleagues and clients.

This period of Maya's life was not just about professional growth; it was also about personal validation. Every long hour, every difficult case, every moment spent poring over law books was a stepping stone towards realizing her dreams. Unlike the ephemeral satisfaction of material gains, Maya's achievements were deeply fulfilling. They were a testament to her hard work, her intelligence, and her unwavering commitment to her principles.

But Maya's success was not solely defined by her career. She maintained a healthy balance in her life, dedicating time to her family, friends, and personal interests. She understood the value of a well-rounded life and refused to let her career consume her. This balance kept her grounded and gave her a sense of peace and contentment that was evident to those around her.

In her world, a solid foundation meant more than just professional accolades; it was about building a life that was rich in meaning and purpose. Maya's approach to her career and life was a reflection of the values instilled in her from a young age – the importance of integrity, the pursuit of excellence, and the belief that true success comes from making a positive impact on the world.

As Maya's career continued to soar, she became a role model for young women aspiring to make their mark in the world. She proved that with hard work and dedication, it was possible to break barriers and achieve one's dreams without sacrificing one's values or personal life.

In this chapter of her life, Maya laid a solid foundation not just for a successful career but for a fulfilling life. Her story was a beacon of hope and inspiration, a reminder that true fulfilment comes from within and that the most significant achievements are those that align with one's deepest values and aspirations.

## ECHOES OF LONELINESS

In the midst of the city's ceaseless rhythm, Julia's life, once a whirlwind of social engagements and romantic escapades, began to resonate with the echoes of loneliness. The realization of her deepening solitude crept upon her slowly, a gradual awakening to the stark emptiness that lay beneath the surface of her glamorous lifestyle.

Julia's days, once filled with the constant companionship of her numerous partners and the buzz of social events, began to lose their lustre. The parties that she frequented, once a source of joy and excitement, now felt hollow. The laughter and music, which used to lift her spirits, now seemed to mock her solitude. In the midst of crowds, she felt more alone than ever, her smiles masking an increasing sense of isolation.

As she moved from one relationship to another, the initial thrill of romance gave way to a predictable pattern of disillusionment. The men in her life, captivated initially by her beauty and charm, soon revealed their fleeting commitment and shallow affection. Julia began to see these relationships for what they were - temporary diversions that left her feeling emptier than before.

In her quieter moments, Julia reflected on her life and choices. She realized that in her relentless pursuit of attention and affection, she had neglected the most crucial relationship of all - the one with herself. She had been so busy trying to fill the void within her with external validation that she had lost touch with her own needs and desires.

The luxury apartment that she called home, a place that once symbolized her success in attracting wealthy partners, now felt like a gilded cage. Its walls echoed with the memories of past relationships, each leaving a residue of unfulfilled promises and unmet needs. The expensive gifts and tokens of affection that adorned her space served as reminders of what she had traded for these material possessions - her sense of self, her peace of mind, and her capacity for genuine connection.

Julia's realization of her deepening solitude was a painful awakening. It forced her to confront the uncomfortable truth that her lifestyle, envied by many, was in reality a façade concealing a profound loneliness. The realization was a turning point, a moment of clarity that illuminated the emptiness of her pursuits and the need for a change.

The echoes of loneliness that now filled Julia's life were not just a sign of what she lacked but a call to embark on a journey of self-discovery. They were an invitation to step back from the relentless pursuit of external validation and to turn inwards, to explore the depths of her own heart and mind in search of something more authentic and lasting.

In the heart of the city that never sleeps, Julia stood at a crossroads, the echoes of her loneliness urging her to choose a different path, one that led not to the superficial allure of fleeting relationships, but to the profound fulfilment of self-acceptance and inner peace.

# CROSSROADS

In the midst of her thriving career and balanced life, Maya arrived at a significant crossroads, one that would add a new dimension to her already fulfilling existence. This turning point came in the form of Dwayne, a man who would challenge and complement her in ways she never anticipated.

Maya met Dwayne at a charity event hosted by her law firm. He was a guest speaker, a successful businessman known for his philanthropic endeavours. Dwayne's speech about corporate responsibility and community service resonated deeply with Maya's own values. After the event, they found themselves in a conversation that flowed effortlessly, a meeting of minds and ideals.

Dwayne was different from anyone Maya had met before. He was ambitious and successful, but his success was tempered by a humility and a deep sense of responsibility to give back to society. He was a single father, raising a young son, a role he spoke of with a mix of pride and tenderness. His life's complexities added layers to his character that Maya found intriguing.

In the weeks that followed, Maya and Dwayne's relationship blossomed. Their dates were a mix of intellectual conversations, shared laughter, and a growing sense of mutual respect and affection.

For Maya, Dwayne represented not just a romantic interest, but a partner who shared her commitment to making a positive impact in the world. As their relationship deepened, Maya found herself at a crossroads.

Her life, so far meticulously planned and focused on her career and personal goals, was now intertwined with another's. Dwayne and his son brought a new perspective to her life, challenging her to consider her future not just as an individual, but as part of a potential family.

This phase in Maya's life was marked by introspection and decisions. She found herself balancing her burgeoning relationship with her career, ensuring that one did not overshadow the other. Maya approached her relationship with the same dedication and thoughtfulness that she applied to her career. She understood the importance of nurturing this new aspect of her life, aware that it could bring a richness and fulfilment beyond her professional achievements.

Dwayne's presence in Maya's life brought new joys and challenges, each helping her to grow and learn more about herself. He was supportive of her career, proud of her achievements, and offered a listening ear and sound advice when she faced challenges. Together, they formed a partnership based on mutual respect, shared values, and a common vision for the future.

The crossroads Maya encountered upon meeting Dwayne was not just about choosing a life partner, but about integrating this new relationship into her already successful and fulfilling life. It was about finding balance, making compromises, and opening her heart to new possibilities. This chapter in Maya's life was a testament to her maturity and her ability to embrace change while staying true to her core values and aspirations.

## THE PRICE REVEALED

As the city lights twinkled like distant stars, Julia found herself confronting the emotional cost of her choices, a reckoning that cast a long shadow over her once carefree existence. The price of her relentless pursuit of fleeting relationships and external validation was now laid bare, revealing a landscape of emotional turmoil and unhealed wounds.

The realization dawned on Julia in the quiet aftermath of yet another failed relationship. Each partner had left a mark, a subtle erosion of her self-esteem and sense of worth. She began to see the pattern in her choices, a cycle of seeking validation through others, only to be left feeling more alone and unworthy. The glamour of her lifestyle could no longer mask the growing void within her.

Julia's reflections brought her to a deeper understanding of the emotional cost of her actions. She acknowledged the way she had used relationships as a means to fill an inner emptiness, a strategy that had only served to deepen her loneliness and self-doubt. The realization was painful, but necessary. It was a moment of stark honesty, a confrontation with the parts of herself she had long ignored.

The impact of her lifestyle extended beyond her romantic life. Friendships had suffered, superficial and transient like her romantic entanglements.

Julia saw how her choices had isolated her, leaving her without a support system of genuine, caring relationships. Her social circle, once a source of pride, now seemed like a hollow echo chamber of her own insecurities.

Julia also faced the reality of her stunted personal growth. In her pursuit of love and admiration, she had neglected her own development, both emotionally and intellectually. She realized she had much to learn about herself, about what it truly meant to be happy and fulfilled. This revelation was a turning point, marking the beginning of a journey towards self-discovery and healing.

As Julia grappled with these revelations, she experienced a range of emotions – regret, sadness, a sense of loss. But within this storm of feelings, there was also a glimmer of hope. The recognition of the price she had paid for her choices was also an opportunity, a chance to change course and seek a more authentic and fulfilling life.

"The Price Revealed" is a chapter of introspection and truth for Julia. It marks the end of an era defined by external validation and the beginning of a new chapter focused on inner growth and self-love. The emotional cost of her past choices becomes the catalyst for a transformative journey, one that promises a deeper understanding of herself and the kind of life she truly desires.

# NEW BEGINNINGS

As the season shifted, bringing with it a fresh bloom of life in the city, Maya and Dwayne's relationship entered a phase of new beginnings, blossoming into something profound and significant. This chapter in Maya's life was marked by the growth of a bond that was nurtured by shared values, mutual respect, and a deepening love.

Maya, always so sure-footed in her professional life, found herself navigating the nuances of a relationship that was quickly becoming central to her existence. Dwayne, with his calm demeanour, unwavering support, and shared vision for a meaningful life, was unlike anyone she had ever known. Together, they embarked on a journey that was as much about discovering each other as it was about understanding themselves.

The progression of their relationship was a dance of balance between independence and partnership. Maya, fiercely self-reliant and accustomed to charting her own course, learned the nuances of sharing her life with someone. Dwayne, a single father with his own set of responsibilities, brought a different, yet complementary, perspective to their union. They navigated this territory with open communication, patience, and an ever-growing trust.

Their time together was filled with moments both mundane and memorable. From quiet evenings spent discussing books and ideas, to attending social events as a couple, every experience served to deepen their connection.

 Maya found joy in the little things – the way Dwayne listened intently to her thoughts, his laughter filling her apartment, or the gentle way he interacted with his son, who was quickly becoming a part of her life as well.

Dwayne's presence in Maya's life also brought new insights. He admired her ambition and dedication but also reminded her of the importance of slowing down and savouring life's simpler pleasures. His grounded nature complemented her driven personality, creating a harmonious balance.

As their relationship matured, so did their understanding of what they could build together. Conversations about the future were filled with possibilities – of a shared home, of journeys they wanted to take, of impacts they wished to make in their community. Their dreams and aspirations, once individual threads, began to weave into a shared tapestry of a future they were eager to create together.

"New Beginnings" in Maya and Dwayne's story was not just about the flourishing of a romantic relationship; it was about the emergence of a partnership that promised growth, learning, and fulfilment. Their journey together was a testament to the idea that love, when rooted in respect, shared values, and mutual growth, can be a powerful force that enhances every aspect of life.

# REFLECTIONS IN THE MIRROR

In the solitude of her apartment, surrounded by the trappings of a life that now felt foreign to her, Julia stood before the mirror, confronting not just her reflection, but her past. It was a moment of reckoning, a time to face the myriad of choices and experiences that had shaped her into the woman she saw in the glass.

Julia's journey into the past was a dive into a deep ocean of memories, each wave bringing with it reflections of her former self. She remembered the young girl who equated love with material gifts, the teenager who sought approval in the eyes of her peers, and the woman who believed that affection and self-worth could be found in the arms of lovers. In the quiet of her room, these memories swirled around her, a mix of regret and understanding.

Confronting her past meant acknowledging the hurt she had experienced and, perhaps more painfully, the hurt she had inflicted on others. There were relationships ended carelessly, feelings disregarded in her pursuit of the next exhilarating romance. Julia had to face the fact that her actions, once thought of as harmless in the pursuit of happiness, had consequences, leaving emotional scars both on herself and those she had been with.

But this journey was not just about facing the pain and the mistakes. It was also about recognizing the moments of strength and resilience she had shown. Julia began to see that her life, though marred by poor choices, also contained instances of courage and determination. She had survived the emotional turmoil, and now she had the opportunity to learn from it and grow.

This introspective journey was a cathartic experience for Julia. She began to understand that her past did not have to dictate her future. The realization that she had the power to change her narrative was both liberating and daunting. It was a call to take responsibility for her life, to make choices that aligned with who she truly wanted to be.

"Reflections in the Mirror" was a pivotal chapter in Julia's story, one where she took the first steps towards healing and self-discovery. Looking into the mirror, she no longer saw just the remnants of her past mistakes and misadventures. Instead, she saw the potential for change, the promise of a new beginning, and the emergence of a woman who was ready to face the world with a newfound understanding of herself.

## BUILDING A LIFE

In the heart of the bustling city, as the seasons changed and the world moved forward, Maya was busy building a life that was a beautiful blend of personal happiness and professional fulfilment. With Dwayne by her side, she found herself crafting a life that was rich in love, purpose, and success.

Maya's career continued to flourish, her reputation as a brilliant and ethical lawyer only growing with each case she undertook. Her success at the law firm was a result of her relentless dedication and her innate ability to navigate the complexities of the legal world with grace and intelligence. She was not just a lawyer; she was a beacon of inspiration, a role model for young women aspiring to make their mark in the professional realm.

But Maya's life was not solely defined by her career achievements. Her relationship with Dwayne had evolved into a deep, meaningful partnership that brought a new dimension of joy and complexity to her life. Together, they navigated the challenges of blending their lives, respecting each other's independence while forging a common path.

Dwayne's son, a bright and curious boy, had become an integral part of Maya's life. She embraced her role in his life with a mix of tenderness and responsibility, forming a bond that was both nurturing and enriching.

The three of them together – Maya, Dwayne, and his son – were a picture of a modern family, built not just on love, but on mutual respect, shared values, and a commitment to support one another.

The balance between her personal life and her career was something Maya managed with careful consideration. She believed in the importance of making a meaningful impact in her work, but not at the expense of her family life. Dinners at home, weekend outings, and quality time with Dwayne and his son were as much a priority as her next big case or professional commitment.

Maya also found fulfilment in using her legal expertise for the greater good. She engaged in pro bono work and became involved in community service, often bringing Dwayne and his son along. These activities were a reflection of her belief in the power of giving back, an ethos she shared with Dwayne.

In this chapter of her life, Maya was building more than just a successful career; she was building a life rich in experiences, relationships, and personal growth. Her journey with Dwayne was a testament to the beauty of finding a partner who not only shared her dreams but was also committed to building a shared life together, one filled with love, mutual respect, and the joy of achieving together.

"Building a Life" is a celebration of Maya's achievements, both in her career and her personal life. It's a story of how dedication, love, and a shared vision can create a life that is fulfilling in every aspect. Maya's story in this chapter is one of harmony between her professional aspirations and her personal happiness, a reminder that with the right partner and a clear sense of purpose, it's possible to have it all.

## FLEETING SHADOWS

In the vibrant tapestry of the city, Julia's journey continued, a path marked by the fleeting shadows of her search for meaning. The realization of the emotional cost of her past choices had set her on a quest for something deeper, something more authentic than the transient pleasures she had known.

Julia's days took on a new rhythm, one less frenetic and more introspective. She withdrew from the social scene that had once been her hunting ground, choosing instead to spend time in solitude or with a few close friends who had stood by her through her transformation. These friends, who had seen beyond the glitter of her glamorous life, became her anchors, supporting her in her quest for a more meaningful existence.

The journey was not without its challenges. Old habits and temptations lurked in the corners of her life, calling to her with the familiar allure of instant gratification and superficial validation. Julia found herself walking a tightrope, balancing between her old world and the new life she yearned to create.

In her pursuit of meaning, Julia turned to activities and pursuits that she had once dismissed. She began to explore her interests, rediscovering passions and hobbies that she had neglected in her pursuit of romance and admiration.

From art classes to volunteering at local charities, each new activity was a step towards understanding herself, towards filling the void with something substantial and real.

Julia also embarked on a journey of self-education. She read extensively, books on philosophy, psychology, and personal development, each page offering insights into the human condition and her own psyche. She began to understand the patterns of her behaviour, the underlying reasons for her relentless pursuit of affection, and the ways in which she could change her life's narrative.

As she delved deeper into this process of self-discovery, Julia began to experience moments of profound clarity and peace. These moments were fleeting, like shadows cast by the clouds on a sunny day, but they were real and powerful. They were glimpses of the life she could have, a life defined not by the men she was with or the parties she attended, but by her own sense of self and purpose.

"Fleeting Shadows" in Julia's story is a chapter of transition, a time of both struggle and awakening. It's a period marked by her search for meaning in a world where she had once found only temporary pleasures. This chapter is a testament to Julia's resilience and her desire to find a deeper, more authentic way of living, a journey that promises to lead her out of the shadows and into a brighter, more meaningful future.

## STABILITY AND LOVE

In the fabric of the bustling city, Maya's life unfolded with a sense of stability and love that she had carefully cultivated. Her relationship with Dwayne had blossomed into a beautiful partnership, culminating in a marriage that was a celebration of shared values, mutual respect, and deep affection.

The wedding was a reflection of both Maya and Dwayne – simple yet elegant, an event that focused more on the commitment they were making to each other than on ostentation. Surrounded by family, friends, and colleagues, they vowed to support and cherish each other, not just in the peaks of joy but through the trials of life.

Marriage brought a new dimension to Maya's personal growth. It was a union that strengthened her, not by diminishing her individuality, but by complementing her strengths with Dwayne's. Together, they were a formidable team, navigating the complexities of life with a combined wisdom and understanding. Maya found in Dwayne not just a husband, but a partner in the truest sense – someone who encouraged her ambitions, shared her passions, and provided a different perspective that enriched her own.

This period of her life was also one of introspection and self-development. Maya's marriage and her role in Dwayne's son's life encouraged her to explore aspects of herself she hadn't known before.

She discovered reservoirs of patience, empathy, and love that added new layers to her personality. Being part of a family taught her about the nuances of relationships, the give and take, and the delicate balance between supporting others and nurturing oneself.

Professionally, Maya continued to excel. Her marriage and the stability it brought to her personal life seemed to fuel her career even further. She became known not just for her legal expertise but also for her ability to balance her professional and personal life with grace. Her achievements were not just accolades and victories in the courtroom; they were the lives she touched, the young lawyers she mentored, and the causes she championed.

"Stability and Love" in Maya's story is a testament to the idea that personal and professional fulfilment can coexist harmoniously. Her marriage to Dwayne was not a hindrance to her career; rather, it was a source of strength that propelled her forward. This chapter of her life was a celebration of love, not just the romantic kind, but a deeper, more holistic love that encompassed all aspects of her life, enriching and elevating her journey in every way.

## BREAKING POINT

In the midst of her quest for meaning and self-discovery, Julia reached a juncture that would test her resolve and push her to the limits of her emotional endurance. This was her breaking point, a personal crisis that shook the very foundations of her newfound path.

The crisis was triggered by an unexpected encounter. One evening, Julia ran into an ex-partner, one who had played a significant role in her life. Seeing him, seemingly happy and content with his new family, stirred a whirlwind of emotions within Julia. Memories of their time together, the good and the bad, flooded back, bringing with them a deluge of regret and what-ifs.

This encounter was a stark reminder of the life she had left behind, a life filled with superficial relationships that had left her feeling empty and unfulfilled. It forced Julia to confront the reality of her choices and the impact they had not only on her life but also on those around her. The realization that she had often been a catalyst for pain and disappointment in her relationships was a bitter pill to swallow.

The days following the encounter were some of the hardest Julia had ever faced. She grappled with feelings of loneliness, unworthiness, and a deep-seated fear that she might never find the sense of belonging and happiness she so desperately sought.

Her journey of self-improvement, which had started with so much
hope, now seemed like an uphill battle, fraught with doubts and
insecurities.

This breaking point forced Julia to pause and re-evaluate her journey.
She spent days in introspection, trying to understand the root of her
pain and how she could move forward. It was during this time of crisis
that Julia realized the importance of facing her issues head-on, rather
than seeking to bury them under new experiences or relationships.

She sought help, turning to counselling as a means to deal with her past
traumas and current emotional turmoil. In therapy, she found a safe
space to express her fears and anxieties, to delve deeper into the
patterns of her behaviour, and to start the process of healing from
within.

"Breaking Point" was a crucial chapter in Julia's story, one that
represented both a low and a turning point. It was a period marked by
pain and introspection, but also by growth and resilience. This chapter
showed that sometimes, it's in our darkest moments that we find the
strength to seek the light, and it's through confronting our deepest
fears that we find the path to true healing and transformation.

# A DIFFERENT WORLD

While Julia navigated through her personal upheavals, Maya's journey took her through a landscape of professional triumphs and milestones. Her world, rooted in stability, love, and ambition, saw her scaling new heights in her career, establishing herself not just as a successful lawyer, but as a beacon of inspiration in her field.

Maya's professional life was a whirlwind of landmark cases, recognition, and achievements. She had become a partner at her law firm, a position that spoke volumes of her expertise, dedication, and the respect she commanded. Her rise through the ranks was not just a testament to her legal acumen but also to her innate ability to lead, inspire, and innovate.

One of Maya's significant achievements was her involvement in a high-profile case that had garnered national attention. The case was complex, involving issues of corporate ethics and social responsibility. Maya's handling of the case, her meticulous attention to detail, and her unwavering commitment to justice earned her accolades not only from her peers but also from the wider community. The success of the case reinforced her belief in the power of the law as a tool for positive change.

But Maya's world was not just about individual success. She was deeply committed to using her position to make a difference. She became a mentor to young lawyers, particularly women, guiding them through the challenges of the legal profession. Her leadership style was a blend of strength and empathy, encouraging her team to strive for excellence while maintaining a healthy work-life balance.

Maya also dedicated herself to various causes, using her legal expertise to advocate for those who lacked a voice. She worked with non-profits, providing pro bono legal counsel, and became a sought-after speaker on issues of law, ethics, and women's empowerment. Her impact extended beyond the courtroom; it was felt in the community and the lives she touched through her work.

In this chapter of her life, Maya's world was a different world from Julia's. It was a world where success was measured not just in victories and accolades but in the positive impact made on society and the people around her. "A Different World" in Maya's story is a narrative of empowerment, leadership, and the realization of one's potential to drive meaningful change.

Maya's professional achievements were a reflection of her character — her integrity, intelligence, and her deep-rooted desire to contribute to a world that was just, fair, and equitable.

This chapter is a celebration of her journey, a tribute to her hard work, and an acknowledgment of the difference one person can make when they are driven by passion, guided by ethics, and supported by a foundation of love and stability.

## AWAKENING

In the solitude of her journey, amidst the turbulence of introspection and the shadows of past choices, Julia arrived at a defining moment – an awakening that brought with it a profound clarity and a renewed sense of purpose.

This moment of clarity did not come as a sudden revelation; rather, it was the culmination of her many days and nights of soul-searching, therapy sessions, and the slow, often painful process of confronting her deepest fears and insecurities. It was as if the pieces of a complex puzzle were finally falling into place, revealing a picture of who Julia was and who she could become.

Julia realized that her search for love and validation from others was a reflection of the love and acceptance she had been denying herself. She understood that the affection she so desperately sought had to come from within, that self-love and self-acceptance were the keys to the fulfilment she craved. This realization was both empowering and humbling; it shifted her perspective from seeking external validation to nurturing her inner well-being.

With this awakening, Julia began to make more conscious choices about her life. She re-evaluated her relationships, choosing to foster connections that were nurturing and genuine.

She found joy in solitude and activities that enriched her soul, such as reading, meditating, and spending time in nature. These activities were not escapes but avenues for her to connect with her true self.

Julia's moment of clarity also brought a change in her career aspirations. She realized that her previous job, which she had chosen for its status and social benefits, was not aligned with her values and passions. Motivated by a desire to make a meaningful contribution, Julia began exploring career paths that were more fulfilling. She considered fields that would allow her to use her experiences to help others, perhaps in counselling or social work.

This chapter of Julia's story, "Awakening," is a poignant narrative of self-discovery and transformation. It marks a significant transition from a life led by external influences to one guided by inner truth. Julia's journey is a testament to the power of self-reflection and the courage it takes to change one's life course.

Her awakening is not just about personal growth; it's a beacon of hope for anyone who finds themselves lost in the labyrinth of their choices. It shows that it's never too late to change, to find clarity, and to live a life that is true to one's self. Julia's story in this chapter is a celebration of the human spirit's resilience and the transformative power of awakening to one's own potential and worth.

## FAMILY TIES

As Maya's professional life continued to soar, her personal life, intertwined with Dwayne and his son, blossomed into a rich tapestry of family ties, each thread representing love, understanding, and mutual growth. This chapter in Maya's life was a warm exploration of her evolving role within this new family dynamic and the joys and challenges it brought.

The heart of Maya and Dwayne's family life was their home, a space that resonated with warmth, laughter, and the occasional chaos typical of a bustling household. Maya, adapting to her role as a stepmother, navigated this new terrain with a combination of empathy, patience, and love. Dwayne's son, initially cautious around Maya, gradually warmed up to her, and they developed a bond that was nurturing and affectionate. Maya discovered in herself a maternal side she hadn't known, filled with protective instincts and a deep capacity for love.

Family dinners became a cherished ritual in their household. These meals were more than just a time to share food; they were moments filled with stories, debates, and discussions about their day. Maya and Dwayne made it a point to encourage open communication, creating an environment where each family member could share their thoughts and feelings freely.

Dwayne and Maya also faced the challenges of blending their families, a task that required understanding and a willingness to adapt. They worked together to build a unified family unit, respecting and honouring each other's past while creating a new future together. Holidays, birthdays, and special occasions were celebrated with a blend of traditions from both their backgrounds, creating new memories and strengthening their family bonds.

Maya's relationship with Dwayne's extended family was another aspect of her family life. She was welcomed with warmth and acceptance, and she, in turn, embraced these new relationships with grace and enthusiasm. Family gatherings were occasions for joy, laughter, and the sharing of stories, further deepening Maya's sense of belonging.

In this chapter of her life, Maya's family ties extended beyond the confines of her immediate household. She maintained a strong connection with her own family, her parents, and siblings, ensuring that they were an integral part of her new life with Dwayne. These family connections provided a support system, a network of love and care that was invaluable.

"Family Ties" in Maya's story is a celebration of the beauty and complexity of family life. It highlights the joys of building a family, the challenges of blending lives, and the profound impact of love and understanding in creating a harmonious household.

This chapter is a testament to Maya's ability to balance her professional success with a rich and fulfilling personal life, proving that one can indeed have it all – a thriving career, a loving partner, and a happy, united family.

## THE JOURNEY INWARD

Amidst the backdrop of the bustling city, Julia embarked on the most crucial journey of her life - the journey inward. This chapter of her story is a profound exploration into the depths of her own psyche, a voyage marked by introspection, healing, and self-discovery.

The catalyst for this inward journey was Julia's moment of awakening, her realization that the key to her fulfilment lay within herself, not in the external world of relationships and social acclaim. This understanding propelled her on a path of self-exploration, a quest to uncover the layers of her identity and to heal the wounds of her past.

Julia's journey began with self-reflection. She spent hours journaling, delving into her thoughts and emotions, unearthing patterns and beliefs that had governed her life. This process was not easy; it required her to confront uncomfortable truths, to face the insecurities and fears that had driven her past behaviours. Yet, with each written word, Julia found a sense of liberation, a release from the chains of her previous self.

Therapy was a cornerstone of Julia's path to self-discovery. In her sessions, she found a safe space to explore her childhood experiences, the relationship with her parents, and the impact these had on her adult life.

Her therapist guided her through various modalities, from cognitive behavioural therapy to mindfulness practices, aiding her in understanding and healing her emotional scars.

Julia also sought solace and growth in activities that nurtured her soul. She found peace in meditation, a practice that allowed her to connect with her inner self and to find a sense of calm amidst the chaos of her thoughts. Yoga became a ritual, not just for physical wellness, but as a means to cultivate balance and harmony within.

This journey inward was also about building a new relationship with herself. Julia learned to practice self-compassion, to forgive herself for her past mistakes, and to embrace her imperfections. She began to appreciate her strengths, to acknowledge her worth, and to set boundaries that protected her well-being.

Julia's exploration of self-led her to rediscover old passions and to find new interests. She reconnected with her love for art, finding joy and expression in painting and sculpture. She also discovered a love for nature, spending time in parks and by the sea, which brought her a sense of peace and grounding.

"The Journey Inward" in Julia's story is a powerful narrative of transformation. It's about stripping away the layers of external validation to reveal the true essence of who she is. This chapter is a testament to the strength it takes to embark on such a journey and the profound changes that can occur when one has the courage to face oneself. Julia's story in this chapter is a beacon of hope for anyone who finds themselves at a crossroads, showing that the journey to self-discovery, while challenging, is perhaps the most rewarding journey one can undertake.

# CHALLENGES MET

As Maya navigated her life, balancing her roles as a partner, stepmother, and a leading lawyer, she encountered a series of challenges that tested her resilience, both professionally and personally. This chapter of her story is a testament to her strength and adaptability in the face of these obstacles.

In her professional life, Maya was confronted with a particularly complex legal case that put her skills and ethics to the test. The case involved a significant corporate client of her firm, embroiled in a legal battle that presented moral dilemmas and a potential conflict of interest. Maya's commitment to justice and her firm's interests were at odds, putting her in a position where she had to make difficult decisions. Navigating this tightrope required not just legal expertise, but a firm adherence to her principles, showcasing her integrity and dedication to the law.

Meanwhile, in her personal life, Maya faced challenges of a different nature. Dwayne's business required him to travel extensively, leaving Maya to juggle her demanding career with her responsibilities at home. This new dynamic brought about a shift in her routine and required a recalibration of her work-life balance. It was a learning curve, understanding how to manage her time effectively while ensuring that her family life did not take a backseat.

Additionally, Maya found herself in the role of a mediator in a family conflict. Dwayne's son, navigating the complexities of adolescence, faced challenges at school and needed guidance and support. Maya stepped into this role with empathy and wisdom, helping to bridge the communication gap between Dwayne and his son. Her ability to handle this sensitive situation strengthened the bonds within their family, but it also brought to light the challenges of parenting and the importance of patience and understanding.

These professional and personal challenges were not just obstacles for Maya; they were opportunities for growth. Each challenge she faced helped to hone her skills, deepen her understanding of herself, and reinforce her values. Maya met each challenge with a combination of intelligence, grace, and resilience, proving to herself and those around her that she was capable of handling the complexities of her multifaceted life.

"Challenges Met" in Maya's story is a narrative of perseverance and adaptability. It shows her ability to confront and overcome obstacles, finding within them the chance to learn and evolve. This chapter is a reflection of the reality that challenges are an integral part of life, and it is through facing them that one discovers their true strength and potential. Maya's journey through these trials is an inspiration, a reminder that life's challenges, while daunting, can lead to significant personal and professional growth.

## SEEKING REDEMPTION

Julia's journey of self-discovery and awakening transitioned into a phase of active change and redemption. This chapter of her life, "Seeking Redemption," is about her efforts to transform her life, to make amends for past mistakes, and to find a path that aligns with her true self.

One of the first steps Julia took in seeking redemption was to reach out to those she had hurt in the past. This was a difficult process, fraught with vulnerability and the potential for rejection. Julia approached her old relationships with a sense of humility, offering sincere apologies and acknowledging the pain she may have caused. While not all of these overtures were met with forgiveness, the act of making them was a crucial step in her path towards healing.

Julia also sought to change the trajectory of her career. The emptiness she had felt in her previous job led her to seek a career that was more in line with her values and newfound understanding of herself. She explored opportunities in fields that allowed her to help others, drawing on her own experiences of transformation and growth. Eventually, Julia found a role in a non-profit organization focused on empowering women, a position that resonated with her journey and allowed her to contribute positively to the lives of others.

In addition to these external changes, Julia's quest for redemption involved a deep internal transformation. She continued her therapy sessions, delving deeper into the roots of her behaviour and working on building self-esteem and self-compassion. Julia also maintained her practices of meditation and mindfulness, which helped her stay centred and aligned with her goals.

Julia's relationships underwent a transformation as well. She became more selective, seeking connections that were based on mutual respect, understanding, and shared values. She learned to enjoy her own company, finding peace in solitude, a stark contrast to her earlier fear of being alone.

Part of Julia's redemption journey was learning to forgive herself. She came to understand that while she could not change her past, she could learn from it and use those lessons to shape a better future. This self-forgiveness was not a one-time event but a continuous process that required her to challenge her self-critical thoughts and to acknowledge her worth and growth.

"Seeking Redemption" in Julia's story is a powerful narrative of change, responsibility, and growth. It shows her commitment to transforming her life, not just superficially, but at a deep, meaningful level.

This chapter is a story of hope and resilience, demonstrating that it is never too late to seek redemption and to make changes that lead to a more authentic and fulfilling life. Julia's journey is a testament to the power of self-reflection, the courage to face one's flaws, and the potential for redemption that lies within all of us.

## PARALLEL LIVES

In the bustling city, the lives of Julia and Maya continued to unfold, parallel yet distinctly different, each woman navigating her own unique journey. "Parallel Lives" is a chapter that juxtaposes their daily experiences, highlighting the contrasts and similarities in their paths towards fulfilment and self-discovery.

Julia's days were now a blend of purposeful activities and introspective moments. Each morning, she would start her day with meditation, a practice that grounded her and provided clarity. Her work at the non-profit organization brought a sense of fulfilment that was new to her; it was a job that aligned with her values and allowed her to make a tangible difference. Her evenings were often spent in therapy sessions or attending workshops and seminars that supported her personal growth. Julia's social life had transformed dramatically; gone were the days of glamorous parties and superficial encounters. Instead, her time was spent with a small, close-knit group of friends who supported and understood her new way of life.

Meanwhile, Maya's days were a dynamic mix of professional challenges and personal joys. Mornings began with a quick, efficient routine, balancing her time between preparing for a busy day at the law firm and spending a few moments with Dwayne and his son. Her work was demanding but deeply rewarding, filled with complex cases and the mentorship of younger lawyers. Evenings in Maya's household were lively, with family dinners, discussions about their days, and planning for upcoming activities and trips. Her weekends often involved community service projects, family outings, or quiet evenings at home, reflecting the balanced life she had cultivated.

The contrast between Julia and Maya's lives was stark. Julia's journey was inward-focused, centred on healing and personal development, a stark change from her previous life. Her world was quieter, more reflective, but rich with the discovery of her authentic self and the pursuit of a life that was truly hers. Maya's life, on the other hand, was outwardly dynamic, a blend of professional success and a fulfilling personal life. Her days were structured yet flexible, busy yet balanced, a testament to her ability to manage multiple roles with grace and effectiveness.

Despite these differences, there were similarities in their journeys. Both women were on paths of self-discovery and growth, each in her own way. Julia's journey was about rebuilding and redefining her life, while Maya's was about expanding and enriching hers. Both were strong, determined women who had faced challenges and were navigating the complexities of life with resilience and grace.

"Parallel Lives" is a chapter that beautifully illustrates the divergent paths that life can take. It's a story of two women, each charting her course, facing her challenges, and seeking fulfilment in her unique way. This chapter shows that while our journeys may differ, the underlying quest for meaning, purpose, and happiness is a shared human experience.

# A NEW DAWN

Julia's story entered a phase of profound transformation, a period aptly termed "A New Dawn." This chapter marks the beginning of a significant shift in her life, as she actively implements the insights and realizations from her journey inward to effect tangible change in her external world.

This transformation was visible in several aspects of Julia's life. Professionally, she embraced her role at the non-profit organization with renewed vigour and purpose. She found herself deeply involved in initiatives that empowered women, drawing from her own experiences to connect and empathize with those she was helping. Her work, once a means to an end, now became a source of genuine satisfaction and pride.

Julia's approach to relationships underwent a dramatic change. Gone were the days of seeking validation through romantic entanglements. Instead, she sought and nurtured friendships that were rooted in mutual respect, understanding, and shared interests. In her romantic life, Julia took a cautious yet open approach. She was no longer in a rush to fill a void but was willing to wait for a partnership that was healthy and fulfilling.

One of the most significant transformations for Julia was in her relationship with herself. She learned to appreciate her own company, finding joy in solitude and quiet moments. Her self-care routines – which included meditation, exercise, and pursuing hobbies like art and literature – were no longer just activities but integral parts of her life that brought her peace and happiness.

Julia also made a conscious effort to give back to the community, participating in volunteer work, and using her experiences to guide and support others. This act of giving back was not only a way to contribute to society but also a means of healing and growth for herself.

The changes in Julia's life were gradual but steady. With each passing day, she grew more in tune with her authentic self, and her life began to reflect this newfound alignment. The sense of fulfilment she now experienced was profoundly different from the fleeting pleasures of her past – it was deeper, more enduring, and genuinely enriching.

"A New Dawn" in Julia's story is a chapter of hope and renewal. It's a testament to the human capacity for change and the power of resilience. Julia's transformation shows that it's possible to emerge from periods of turmoil and confusion with a clearer sense of self and a renewed purpose. This chapter is a celebration of her journey towards a life that is not only more meaningful but also more reflective of who she truly is.

# THE TEST OF TIME

As the seasons changed and years passed, Maya and Dwayne's relationship, deeply rooted in love, respect, and shared values, faced the inevitable test of time. "The Test of Time" is a chapter that explores the evolution of their relationship as it matures and adapts to the changing tides of life.

Throughout this period, Maya and Dwayne's bond was strengthened by the challenges they faced together. They navigated the complexities of raising a teenager, with Dwayne's son growing into his own person, bringing with it the typical challenges of adolescence. Maya's role in his life had now become more significant, and together with Dwayne, they formed a united front, guiding and supporting him through these formative years.

Professionally, both Maya and Dwayne reached new heights in their careers. Maya's growing responsibilities at the law firm and her involvement in community service, coupled with Dwayne's business successes, meant that their lives were busier than ever. This brought about the challenge of finding quality time together, making them more intentional about nurturing their relationship. They made sure to set aside time for each other, whether it was a quiet dinner at home, a weekend getaway, or simply moments of connection amidst their hectic schedules.

One significant aspect of their evolving relationship was their ability to support each other's growth and aspirations. Dwayne was a pillar of support for Maya's career, celebrating her achievements and providing comfort during setbacks. Similarly, Maya was a sounding board for Dwayne, offering insights and advice, and sharing in the joys and challenges of his business ventures.

Their communication, always a cornerstone of their relationship, deepened further. They learned to navigate disagreements and misunderstandings with patience and understanding, always keeping the lines of communication open and honest. This ability to discuss and resolve issues was a crucial factor in the longevity and health of their relationship.

As they grew individually and as a couple, Maya and Dwayne also revisited and realigned their shared goals and dreams. They planned for the future, considering everything from family decisions to personal ambitions, ensuring that their journey together was in harmony with their individual paths.

"The Test of Time" in Maya and Dwayne's story is a testament to the enduring nature of their relationship. It highlights the importance of mutual support, effective communication, and shared values in sustaining a long-term partnership.

This chapter is a celebration of enduring love, showcasing how a relationship can evolve and grow stronger over time, facing challenges not as obstacles but as opportunities to deepen and enrich the bond.

## CROSSING PATHS

In a serendipitous twist of fate, the lives of Julia and Maya, which had been running parallel yet separate, intersected, weaving a new thread into the tapestry of their stories. "Crossing Paths" is a chapter that unfolds this unexpected meeting, a moment that marks the convergence of their distinct journeys.

The intersection occurred at a community event focused on women's empowerment, a cause close to both their hearts. Maya was a guest speaker, sharing her insights on women's roles in the legal profession and the importance of mentorship. Julia, actively involved in her non-profit work, was attending the event to network and learn.

As Maya spoke eloquently on the stage, Julia was in the audience, listening intently. She was struck by Maya's poise, intelligence, and the passion with which she spoke about her work and the empowerment of women. After the talk, Julia felt compelled to meet Maya, to express her admiration and to discuss potential collaborations between their organizations.

The meeting between Julia and Maya was a moment of mutual recognition - not of each other's pasts, but of their shared values and commitments to making a difference in the lives of women.

They talked at length, finding common ground in their work and perspectives. This interaction sparked a connection, an acknowledgment of each other as allies in their respective missions.

From this initial meeting, a professional relationship blossomed. Maya found Julia's insights from her work in the non-profit sector invaluable, while Julia respected Maya's accomplishments and her dedication to using her position to effect positive change. Their interactions, though primarily professional, were underpinned by a growing mutual respect and understanding.

As they collaborated on various initiatives and projects, their relationship evolved into a friendship. They discovered similarities in their journeys - their quests for personal growth, the challenges they had faced and overcome, and their aspirations for the future. This bond enriched their lives, providing a new dimension of support and camaraderie.

"Crossing Paths" is a chapter that highlights the beauty of unexpected connections and the power of shared goals and visions. It's a narrative about how lives can intersect at just the right moment, leading to meaningful relationships that have the capacity to enrich and inspire. For Julia and Maya, this intersection was not just a chance meeting; it was a convergence of paths that added depth and richness to their personal and professional journeys.

# REVELATIONS

In the unfolding story of Julia's transformation and new beginnings, a chapter emerged that brought her face-to-face with her past. "Revelations" is a poignant narrative of how Julia's previous life collides with her present, forcing her to confront unresolved issues and secrets long buried.

The catalyst for these revelations was an unexpected encounter with a figure from her past – a former partner who had played a significant role in her life during her years of turmoil. This individual reappeared not with old romantic intentions, but with news that challenged Julia's newfound stability: the existence of a child, a daughter, born from their relationship and given up for adoption years ago.

This shocking discovery sent ripples through Julia's world. The knowledge of having a child, one she had been unaware of, brought a mix of emotions – guilt for not being there, sadness for the lost years, and a profound confusion about what to do next. This revelation also brought a sense of responsibility and an urgent desire to make things right, to somehow be a part of her daughter's life.

As Julia grappled with this new reality, she sought counsel from her therapist and close friends. They provided her with support and guidance, helping her navigate the complex emotions and decisions that lay ahead.

Julia knew that any steps she took would have significant implications, not just for her but for her daughter and the family who had raised her.

This chapter of Julia's life also entailed reaching out and establishing a connection with her daughter. The process was delicate and fraught with uncertainty. Julia approached it with a deep respect for her daughter's feelings and the life she had with her adoptive family. The initial meetings were emotional, a mix of curiosity, apprehension, and a cautious hope for some form of relationship in the future.

"Revelations" is a chapter that tests Julia's resilience and the strength of her personal growth. It confronts her with the unforeseen consequences of her past actions and challenges her to extend her journey of redemption to include not just herself but others who were unwittingly part of her past choices.

For Julia, this chapter is a profound journey of facing truths, of understanding the far-reaching impacts of our actions, and of learning to forge new connections from the fragments of the past. It's a story of reconciliation and the complex, often painful journey towards healing and forming new bonds. This chapter adds a profound layer to Julia's story, showing how our past can shape our future in ways we never anticipate, and how courage and compassion can guide us through even the most unexpected turns in life.

# A SHARED JOURNEY

In the evolving narrative of Julia's life, particularly as she faced the unexpected revelation of her long-lost daughter, Maya became an unexpected source of support and guidance. "A Shared Journey" is a chapter that delves into the deepening of Julia and Maya's friendship, illustrating how shared experiences and understanding can forge strong bonds.

As Julia navigated the emotional complexities of connecting with her daughter, Maya stood by her side, not just as a friend but as a confidante and advisor. With her background in law and her personal experience in managing delicate family dynamics, Maya was uniquely positioned to offer Julia practical advice and emotional support.

Maya's approach to helping Julia was grounded in empathy and understanding. She listened without judgment, offered insights when appropriate, and shared her experiences in dealing with sensitive family matters. This support was invaluable to Julia, who, despite her progress in therapy and personal growth, found herself overwhelmed by the magnitude of the situation.

The support extended beyond conversations and advice. Maya helped Julia navigate the legal aspects of her situation, offering to connect her with colleagues who specialized in family law and adoption cases. She also encouraged Julia to continue her therapy, emphasizing the importance of professional guidance in such a complex emotional journey.

This phase of their friendship also allowed Maya to reflect on her own life. Supporting Julia provided her with a deeper appreciation for the stability and love she had found in her own family. It reinforced her belief in the power of resilience and the importance of facing challenges head-on.

For Julia, Maya's support was more than just practical help; it was a lifeline during one of the most turbulent periods of her life. Maya's unwavering presence and understanding helped Julia maintain her strength and clarity as she worked to build a relationship with her daughter.

"A Shared Journey" in the story of Julia and Maya is a celebration of the power of friendship and the impact it can have on our lives. It's a testament to how, even in our darkest times, the compassion and support of a friend can help light the way forward.

This chapter beautifully captures the essence of their friendship - one that is rooted in mutual respect, shared experiences, and a deep understanding of each other's journeys. It underscores the idea that sometimes, it's the shared paths in our journey that leave the most significant impact on our lives.

# FACING THE PAST

In Julia's transformative journey, a crucial chapter unfolds as she bravely confronts her history. "Facing the Past" is a poignant narrative about Julia's courageous confrontation with the choices and events of her earlier life, and how this confrontation becomes a pivotal step in her healing process.

This chapter sees Julia revisiting the defining moments and relationships of her past, a task filled with emotional challenges. She reflects on her younger self with a mix of compassion and regret, recognizing the misguided search for love and validation that had guided her actions. This introspection involves not just recalling her relationships but also examining the deeper motivations behind her choices, the unresolved needs from her childhood, and the impact of her parents' emotional absence.

Confronting her history also means acknowledging the pain she had caused others. Julia reaches out to some of her past partners, not seeking to rekindle any relationship, but to express her remorse and to understand the impact of her actions from their perspectives. These conversations are difficult and sometimes confrontational, but they offer a form of closure and understanding that is crucial for her growth.

Julia's therapy sessions intensify during this period, providing a safe and supportive space for her to process the emotions that surface. Her therapist guides her through various exercises and discussions, helping her to dismantle the negative beliefs about herself that had been built over the years and to replace them with a sense of self-compassion and worthiness.

An important aspect of facing her past is Julia's journey of self-forgiveness. She learns to accept that while she cannot change what happened, she can change how she views her past and how she allows it to influence her future. This process is not linear or easy; it involves setbacks and moments of doubt, but Julia remains committed to moving forward.

As Julia confronts her history, she also starts to piece together a new narrative for her life, one that acknowledges her past but is not defined by it. She embraces the lessons learned from her experiences and starts to envision a future that is shaped by her new understanding of herself and her relationships.

"Facing the Past" in Julia's story is a deeply emotional chapter, underscored by resilience and the pursuit of personal redemption. It highlights the often challenging but necessary process of confronting our history to truly move forward.

Julia's journey through this chapter is a powerful testament to the strength it takes to face our past, the healing that comes from acknowledgment and remorse, and the transformative power of self-forgiveness and growth.

## HEALING BONDS

As Julia navigated the complexities of reconciling with her past, her friendship with Maya evolved into a source of strength and healing. "Healing Bonds" is a chapter that explores the deepening relationship between Julia and Maya, highlighting how their bond becomes a catalyst for healing and growth for both women.

The friendship that had initially blossomed from professional respect and shared interests now grew into a profound connection. Maya, with her empathetic nature and stable presence, became a pillar of support for Julia. She was there to listen when Julia needed to talk, offering wisdom and comfort during moments of doubt and frustration. Maya's own experiences and insights provided a perspective that was invaluable to Julia's journey of healing.

For Maya, the friendship with Julia also became a source of growth and enrichment. Julia's resilience and determination in facing her past challenges inspired Maya, reminding her of the power of personal transformation. The openness and vulnerability Julia displayed in sharing her journey encouraged Maya to reflect on her own life, appreciate her blessings, and recognize the strength in her own struggles.

Their conversations often delved into topics of personal development, self-care, and the challenges of womanhood. They shared books, attended workshops together, and even participated in retreats that focused on personal growth and mindfulness. These shared experiences not only strengthened their bond but also provided them with new tools and insights to navigate their respective lives.

The friendship between Julia and Maya also extended beyond their personal development endeavours. They spent time together in more casual settings, enjoying cultural events, exploring new restaurants, or simply spending an evening chatting over coffee. These moments of relaxation and enjoyment were as crucial to their friendship as the more profound discussions they shared.

As they both navigated their individual challenges – Julia with her journey of self-discovery and reconciliation with her past, and Maya with her busy professional life and family responsibilities – their friendship offered a space of mutual understanding and unconditional support. "Healing Bonds" is a chapter that beautifully illustrates the power of friendship in the journey of healing and personal growth. It shows how the bond between Julia and Maya becomes a source of strength and inspiration for both, a reminder of the transformative power of connection, empathy, and shared experiences. This chapter is a celebration of the healing power of friendship and its role in our journeys towards becoming our best selves.

## UNVEILING TRUTHS

In the ongoing journey of Julia's self-discovery, a significant chapter unfolds as she unveils deeper truths about herself. "Unveiling Truths" is a narrative of introspection and revelation, where Julia delves beneath the surface of her past behaviours and attitudes to uncover the core beliefs and experiences shaping her identity.

This chapter sees Julia engaging in a deeper level of self-analysis, often facilitated by her ongoing therapy sessions. She begins to uncover and challenge long-held beliefs about herself, her worth, and her relationships. This process involves revisiting her childhood experiences, understanding the impact of her upbringing, and recognizing how these early influences had set the stage for her adult relationships and self-perception.

Julia confronts some hard truths, particularly about her reliance on external validation and her patterns of seeking affection in unhealthy ways. She acknowledges the defensive mechanisms she had developed over the years – her tendency to shield herself from emotional vulnerability and the persona she had created to gain approval and avoid rejection.

One of the most profound revelations for Julia is recognizing her own strengths and resilience.  Amidst the reflection on past mistakes and wounds, she discovers an inner fortitude she had previously overlooked. This recognition brings a new sense of self-respect and an appreciation for the journey she has undertaken.

Julia also begins to understand the importance of self-compassion. She learns to view her past not with judgment and regret but as a series of experiences that, while painful, have contributed to her growth and understanding. This shift in perspective is crucial in her journey, allowing her to embrace her past while moving forward with hope and confidence.

As she unveils these truths about herself, Julia's relationships evolve. She becomes more authentic in her interactions, no longer driven by the need to impress or appease others. Her friendships deepen, and she approaches the possibility of romantic relationships with a new set of expectations – seeking connections that are genuine, respectful, and nurturing.

"Unveiling Truths" in Julia's story is a powerful testament to the transformative process of self-discovery. It illustrates the courage required to face oneself honestly and the liberation that comes from understanding and accepting one's true self.

This chapter is a celebration of the journey towards self-awareness and the profound impact it has on one's life and relationships. It underscores the idea that by unveiling the deeper truths about ourselves, we can find a more authentic and fulfilling way to live.

# RESILIENCE

As Maya's story progresses, a chapter unfolds that tests her strength and showcases her remarkable resilience in the face of adversity. "Resilience" is a narrative about how Maya confronts and overcomes various challenges, reaffirming her inner strength and steadfast spirit.

A significant challenge arises in Maya's professional life. She is faced with a highly complex and politically sensitive case that puts her under immense pressure. The case not only demands her legal expertise but also tests her ethical boundaries and personal beliefs. Despite the pressure and the high stakes involved, Maya remains committed to her principles, demonstrating her unwavering integrity and dedication to justice.

In her personal life, Maya faces a different kind of challenge. Dwayne's business encounters difficulties, creating tension and stress that spills over into their home life. Maya, in her supportive role, helps Dwayne navigate these troubles, providing both emotional support and practical advice. Her ability to remain composed and optimistic during this turbulent period serves as a pillar of strength for her family.

Additionally, Maya deals with the challenges of parenthood. As Dwayne's son enters his teenage years, new parenting obstacles emerge. Maya's approach to these challenges is a blend of empathy, firmness, and open communication.

Her resilience is evident in her ability to adapt her parenting style to meet the evolving needs of a teenager while maintaining a loving and supportive home environment.

Maya's resilience is also tested by the balancing act of managing her demanding career and her commitments at home. She often finds herself stretched thin, but her organizational skills, along with her ability to prioritize and delegate, help her navigate these demands without compromising on her performance at work or her presence at home.

Throughout these challenges, Maya draws strength from her self-care practices, her strong support system, and her deep-seated belief in her abilities and values. She leans on her friendships, especially her growing bond with Julia, for encouragement and perspective.

"Resilience" in Maya's story is a powerful depiction of her capacity to withstand and rise above adversity. It illustrates how resilience is not about avoiding difficulties but facing them head-on with courage, grace, and an unwavering commitment to one's values and goals. This chapter is a tribute to Maya's strength and adaptability, highlighting how adversity can serve as a catalyst for growth and self-discovery. Maya's journey through these challenges is inspiring, a reminder of the resilience that lies within each of us to overcome the trials we encounter in our lives.

# A NEW CHAPTER

In the evolving narrative of Julia's life, a significant transition occurs, marking the beginning of a brighter and more hopeful phase. "A New Chapter" is a testament to Julia's growth and the positive turn her life takes as a result of her relentless pursuit of self-improvement and healing.

One of the most significant developments in this chapter is Julia's deepening relationship with her daughter. Their bond, initially tentative and fraught with uncertainty, grows stronger as they spend more time together. Julia navigates this new role with sensitivity and patience, respecting the boundaries set by her daughter and her adoptive family. The joy and fulfilment she find in this evolving relationship are profound, filling a part of her heart she didn't realize was empty.

Professionally, Julia finds a new sense of purpose and satisfaction in her work at the non-profit organization. She spearheads several successful initiatives that make a tangible impact on the community, particularly in empowering women who have faced challenges similar to her own. Her experiences and the lessons she has learned become valuable tools in her work, allowing her to connect with and inspire others. Julia also experiences a revival in her personal life. Her circle of friends expands, now including individuals who share her interests and values.

She finds joy in simple pleasures – book clubs, art exhibitions, and nature hikes. Her social life, once a whirlwind of parties and superficial connections, is now more about meaningful interactions and shared experiences.

Another positive development in Julia's life is the prospect of a new romantic relationship. Unlike her past encounters, this relationship evolves slowly and is based on mutual respect, shared interests, and emotional connection. Julia approaches this new relationship with a sense of calm and maturity, reflective of her personal growth and her newfound understanding of what a healthy relationship entails.

Julia's journey in "A New Chapter" is characterized by balance and contentment. She has learned to appreciate her own company and finds joy in her independence. Her approach to life is more mindful and intentional, focusing on activities and relationships that enrich her life and align with her values.

This chapter in Julia's story is about hope, renewal, and the positive changes that come from facing one's challenges head-on. It is a celebration of her resilience, her capacity for change, and her ability to write a new chapter in her life, one that is filled with happiness, purpose, and fulfilment. Julia's story in this phase is a powerful reminder that it is never too late to turn the page and start anew, creating a life that resonates with one's true self.

# FULL CIRCLE

Julia's transformative journey reaches a pivotal point in "Full Circle," a chapter that encapsulates her redemption and remarkable growth. This phase of her story is a powerful illustration of how she comes to terms with her past, embraces her present, and looks forward to a future shaped by her newfound wisdom and self-awareness.

This chapter sees Julia achieving a sense of wholeness she had never experienced before. The reconciliation with her past, particularly the acceptance and integration of her daughter into her life, brings a profound sense of closure and fulfilment. Julia's relationship with her daughter is not just a connection rekindled; it's a testament to her growth and her ability to embrace life's complexities with grace and love.

Julia's professional life flourishes as she becomes a key figure in her organization. Her initiatives and programs, driven by her personal experiences and insights, make significant impacts. She becomes a respected voice in the community, not just for her work but for her story of transformation and resilience.

The redemption arc in Julia's life is also evident in her personal relationships. Her friendships are deeper and more meaningful, characterized by mutual support and genuine connection.

The romantic relationship that had cautiously begun in the previous chapter evolves into a significant and healthy part of her life, adding another layer of joy and companionship.

Perhaps the most remarkable aspect of Julia's full circle is her inner peace and self-acceptance. She has learned to embrace her imperfections, to celebrate her strengths, and to view her life experiences as valuable lessons rather than regrets. This acceptance has brought a level of self-assuredness and contentment that radiates in all aspects of her life.

Julia also finds joy in giving back, in sharing her journey with others who may be facing similar struggles. She becomes involved in speaking engagements, mentorship programs, and community workshops, where her story serves as an inspiration and a beacon of hope.

"Full Circle" in Julia's narrative is not just about redemption; it's about the completion of a journey that transforms adversity into strength, sorrow into joy, and turmoil into peace. It's a chapter that celebrates the power of personal growth and the possibility of change at any stage in life. Julia's story, coming full circle, is a poignant reminder of the human capacity for resilience, change, and the ability to craft a life filled with purpose, love, and fulfilment.

# UNEXPECTED CONNECTIONS

In a surprising twist, "Unexpected Connections" reveals a previously unknown link between Dwayne and Julia, adding a layer of complexity and intrigue to their stories. This chapter delves into the unforeseen intersections of their pasts, unveiling how small the world can be and how interconnected our lives are.

The revelation comes to light during a casual conversation between Maya and Julia, where they share stories about their pasts. As Julia recounts her experiences and the people who played significant roles in her past, Maya begins to recognize a familiar pattern. The details about one particular individual in Julia's past - his personality, career trajectory, and timeline - strikingly match those of Dwayne.

After piecing together more information and confirming with Dwayne, they discover that Dwayne was indeed one of Julia's past acquaintances. This revelation shocks both Maya and Julia, as neither had any inkling of this connection when they first met and became friends. Dwayne had been a part of Julia's life during her years of tumultuous relationships, although their encounter had been brief and not as impactful as her other relationships.

This unexpected connection brings a mix of emotions for everyone involved. For Julia, it's a jarring reminder of her past life, stirring up memories she had worked hard to move beyond. For Maya, it introduces an unforeseen link between her husband and her friend, which she needs to process and understand. And for Dwayne, it's a look back into a chapter of his life that he had since closed.

The revelation, however, is handled with maturity and understanding by all parties. Julia and Dwayne acknowledge their past with a sense of closure and mutual respect for the individuals they have become. Maya, demonstrating her unwavering trust and open-mindedness, navigates this revelation with grace, seeing it as a curious coincidence rather than a threat to their relationships.

"Unexpected Connections" is a chapter about the unpredictability of life and the intertwined nature of human experiences. It highlights how past and present can collide in unexpected ways and how such revelations can test the strength and resilience of relationships.

This chapter is a testament to the understanding, trust, and maturity of Julia, Maya, and Dwayne, illustrating that the past doesn't have to dictate the present and that people can grow and change, forging new paths and relationships that are independent of their history.

# CONVERGENCE OF PATHS

"Convergence of Paths" marks a pivotal point in the narratives of Julia and Maya, where their individual journeys intertwine to create a rich and dynamic tapestry of shared experiences, mutual support, and collaborative endeavours. This chapter celebrates the full integration of their lives, both personally and professionally, demonstrating the profound impact of their friendship.

As Julia solidifies her place in her daughter's life and continues to make significant strides in her professional world, Maya becomes an integral part of this evolution. They collaborate on various projects that blend Julia's non-profit initiatives with Maya's legal expertise, creating programs that empower women and advocate for social justice. Their combined efforts lead to ground-breaking work that has a lasting impact on the community, showcasing the power of partnership and shared vision.

In their personal lives, the friendship between Julia and Maya deepens. They become confidantes, sharing not just successes and professional aspirations but also personal challenges and family life. Maya's insight and stability provide a grounding influence for Julia, while Julia's journey of transformation and resilience offer inspiration and encouragement to Maya.

The intertwining of their paths also brings their families together. Social gatherings, celebrations, and casual meet-ups become common, allowing their loved ones to form connections as well. Dwayne and Julia, linked by a past that is now just a footnote, develop a respectful acquaintance. Simultaneously, Maya forms a bond with Julia's daughter, offering another layer of support and mentorship.

This convergence also brings about opportunities for joint self-development and exploration. Julia and Maya engage in retreats, seminars, and workshops, not just as participants but also as contributors, sharing their stories and insights with wider audiences. Their experiences become a source of inspiration for many, exemplifying the strength found in supportive female friendships.

"Convergence of Paths" is a celebration of the journey Julia and Maya have undertaken, both individually and together. It is a testament to the notion that when paths intertwine, they can lead to unexpected and enriching destinations.

This chapter is a tribute to the power of friendship, collaboration, and the shared journey of growth and empowerment. It underscores the idea that our lives, when connected with those of others, can lead to greater impact, deeper understanding, and more fulfilling experiences.

# THE FINAL REVELATION

In a story filled with growth, healing, and unexpected connections, "The Final Revelation" presents a poignant moment for Julia as she comes to terms with her past connection to Dwayne. This chapter delves into Julia's process of acknowledging and understanding this piece of her history, a step that marks a significant point in her journey of self-discovery and acceptance.

The revelation about her brief past with Dwayne, initially a source of surprise and discomfort, gradually becomes an opportunity for Julia to reflect on the vast changes she has undergone in her life. This introspection is not about dwelling on the past, but about acknowledging it as a part of her journey that has led her to where she is now.

Julia's recognition of her past with Dwayne brings a range of emotions. There is a sense of irony in how their paths had crossed long before she formed a deep friendship with Maya, and a realization of how small and interconnected the world can be.

However, with her newfound maturity and perspective, Julia views this connection as just one of many encounters in her life, each having contributed to her growth in some way.

This revelation also prompts a conversation between Julia and Dwayne, where they acknowledge their brief history. The conversation is marked by mutual respect and an understanding of the different people they were at that time. For Julia, this exchange is affirming; it reinforces her progress and the distance she has come from the person she once was.

For Maya, who facilitates this conversation and supports both parties through it, this revelation serves as a testament to the strength and trust in her relationships with both Julia and Dwayne. It highlights the openness and honesty that underpins her marriage and her friendship, and the mature way in which all parties handle the situation.

"The Final Revelation" is a chapter about coming full circle, about facing the past with a sense of closure and peace. It demonstrates how understanding and accepting our history is a crucial part of personal growth.

This chapter, while revisiting a piece of Julia's past, is less about the events that transpired and more about the person she has become. It symbolizes the end of one chapter in Julia's life and the beginning of another, marked by deeper self-awareness, stronger relationships, and a future that looks bright with possibilities.

# NEW BEGINNINGS, OLD ENDS

"New Beginnings, Old Ends" is a pivotal chapter in the narratives of Julia and Maya, encapsulating the theme of resolution and the commencement of new chapters in their lives. This chapter eloquently weaves the conclusion of past conflicts with the onset of fresh starts, symbolizing a period of closure and renewal.

For Julia, resolving past conflicts involves a series of conscious efforts to make peace with her history. This includes not only her recent revelation regarding Dwayne but also her broader past of tumultuous relationships and the emotional baggage they carried. She reaches out to key figures from her past, seeking to understand and, where possible, mend old wounds. This process is challenging and emotional, yet necessary for her to move forward without the weight of unresolved issues.

Simultaneously, Julia embarks on a new journey in her professional and personal life. Her role at the non-profit organization takes on new significance, with initiatives that draw on her experiences and her journey of transformation. In her personal life, her relationship with her daughter blossoms, and the new romantic relationship she has nurtured offers a promising future, filled with mutual respect and shared values.

Maya, on the other hand, finds resolution in balancing the different facets of her life more harmoniously. The challenges she faced in her professional life and the pressures of her personal life find a more stable equilibrium. She learns to delegate more, to trust in the abilities of her team, and to create space for her family and herself. This period also marks a time of growth in her relationship with Dwayne, as they successfully navigate the complexities of their past and present, emerging stronger and more united.

Additionally, Maya's role as a mentor and leader in her professional sphere evolves. She becomes more involved in initiatives aimed at empowering young women in the legal field, drawing inspiration from her friendship with Julia and their shared experiences.

"New Beginnings, Old Ends" is a chapter about the beauty of closure and the excitement of new possibilities. It highlights the importance of addressing and resolving past conflicts to fully embrace the future. For Julia and Maya, this chapter marks a significant phase in their lives where they are able to let go of the past, learn from it, and step into new beginnings with confidence and hope. It's a testament to the idea that endings are often necessary precursors to new beginnings, and that in resolving our past conflicts, we open ourselves up to new opportunities and experiences.

# COMING TOGETHER

"Coming Together" is a heart-warming chapter in the lives of Julia and Maya, where their individual journeys lead to a harmonious union of their families, symbolizing unity, acceptance, and collective growth. This chapter narrates how their friendship serves as a bridge, bringing together not just two women but two families, each moving forward into a shared future.

As Julia's relationship with her daughter strengthens, she gradually introduces her to her new life, including her friendship with Maya. This introduction marks the beginning of a series of gatherings where both families start to interact and bond. Maya and Dwayne, with their open-heartedness and warmth, welcome Julia and her daughter into their family circle. These gatherings are filled with moments of laughter, shared stories, and the building of new memories.

For Dwayne's son, these interactions are an opportunity to connect with Julia's daughter, forming a new friendship that adds another layer to the family dynamics. The children, despite their different backgrounds, find common ground and mutual understanding, mirroring the journey their parents have undergone.

These familial interactions are not without their challenges, as blending different personalities and histories often is. However, the prevailing atmosphere is one of mutual respect and a willingness to understand

and embrace each other's differences. Julia and Maya, with their shared experiences and the strength of their friendship, act as anchors for their families, guiding them through the process of coming together.

A significant moment in this chapter is a joint celebration, perhaps a holiday or a special event, where both families come together to celebrate their unity and newfound relationships. This event symbolizes the culmination of their journey of coming together - a joyous affirmation of their bond and a hopeful look towards the future.

"Coming Together" is a chapter that celebrates the power of human connection and the beauty of forming new familial bonds. It highlights how friendships can transcend individual relationships and foster wider connections, creating extended families bound not by blood, but by choice, respect, and love. This chapter in the lives of Julia and Maya is a testament to the idea that families are not just formed by birth but can be created through shared experiences, empathy, and the willingness to embrace each other's stories and journeys.

## LEGACY OF CHOICES

"Legacy of Choices" serves as the reflective and forward-looking finale to the intertwining stories of Julia and Maya. This chapter encapsulates the culmination of their experiences, the decisions they've made, and the paths they've chosen, while also casting an eye toward the future and the legacy of these choices.

For Julia, this chapter is a time of contemplation on how her choices, both past and present, have shaped her life. From the turbulence of her younger years to the more grounded and purposeful life she leads now, every decision has contributed to her growth and understanding. She reflects on the impact of her choices on her daughter, recognizing that her journey of self-discovery and redemption has not only transformed her own life but has also laid the foundation for a healthier, more open relationship with her child. Julia looks ahead with a sense of hope and determination, committed to continuing her path of personal development and to being a positive influence in the lives of those she touches.

Maya, on the other hand, reflects on her journey with a sense of gratitude and accomplishment. Her choices, rooted in integrity and a deep sense of responsibility, have led to a fulfilling career, a loving family, and a meaningful friendship with Julia. She acknowledges the challenges she's faced and how they've strengthened her.

Looking to the future, Maya is excited about the possibilities that lie ahead - both for her own growth and for the impact she can continue to have through her work and her mentoring of young women.

The friendship between Julia and Maya, central to this chapter, is a testament to the power of supportive relationships in personal growth and resilience. They look back on their journey together with a deep understanding of how their friendship has enriched their lives. They recognize that their legacy is not only in the choices they've made but also in the strength and wisdom they've drawn from each other.

"Legacy of Choices" is not just a conclusion but a gateway to future possibilities. It underscores the idea that our lives are a tapestry woven from the threads of our choices, each decision contributing to the pattern that emerges. For Julia and Maya, the legacy of their choices is a narrative of strength, growth, and the enduring power of friendship. It's a reminder that while our paths may be shaped by our past, they are also filled with the potential for continued growth, change, and the creation of a positive legacy for the future.

# EPILOGUE

As the story of Julia and Maya draws to a close, the epilogue offers a reflective and hopeful glimpse into their futures, encapsulating the enduring impact of their journeys and the paths that lie ahead.

Julia's life, once a whirlwind of uncertainty and emotional turmoil, has settled into a rhythm of contentment and purpose. Her relationship with her daughter is a source of immense joy and continual learning. Professionally, Julia has become a beacon of hope and inspiration in her community, using her experiences to empower others. She has also found love in a partner who respects and supports her journey. Julia's past, with its trials and tribulations, now serves as a powerful testimony to her resilience and capacity for transformation.

Maya, in her balanced world of career, family, and friendship, continues to thrive. Her role as a mentor and advocate for women in the legal field grows ever more influential, inspiring a new generation of female lawyers. Her marriage with Dwayne remains strong, rooted in mutual respect and shared dreams. The challenges they faced together have only deepened their bond. Maya's life is a testament to the power of integrity, hard work, and the impact one individual can have on the lives of many.

The friendship between Julia and Maya stands as a central pillar in both their lives. It has evolved into more than just a source of support; it's a celebration of shared experiences and mutual growth. They continue to inspire and learn from each other, their bond a constant reminder of the strength found in connection and understanding.

As we look ahead, the futures of Julia and Maya are bright with promise. Julia's journey of self-discovery and redemption, and Maya's unwavering dedication to her principles and loved ones, pave the way for continued growth and fulfilment. Their stories, intertwined yet distinct, are testaments to the enduring power of resilience, the beauty of transformation, and the strength of friendship.

In this epilogue, we see that the legacy of Julia and Maya's choices extends beyond their individual lives. It's a legacy that inspires those around them and resonates with anyone who has faced adversity, sought change, or endeavoured to live a life true to themselves. Their journeys remind us that while life may present challenges, it also offers endless possibilities for growth, connection, and the creation of a meaningful legacy.

~~~~~~~~~~~~~~~~~~~~~~~**END**~~~~~~~~~~~~~~~~~~~~~~~
~~~~~~~~~~~~~~~~~~~~~~~